CHAPTER I (JAMES)

It is 06h00. The sound of James's alarm echoes in his room as it does every weekday morning. He awakes with an urge, like every other morning, to end his misery. An urge he knows he will one day succumb to. On some mornings this urge is stronger than it is on others. On these dreary mornings, tearing himself away from the safety of sleep into the unpredictable reality of this insufficient life seems to be a monumental task. This morning, May 2nd, 2005, is slightly better than most of the others. Tiny drops of rain crash against his bedroom window in a war-like fashion. The rain has become so comforting to him. There is something sinister about the roaring thunder and the ominous air that the rain brings with her that makes this 16 year old boy feel vulnerable and helpless, it makes him feel weak: human.

Humans are seldom sure about things, living their short and at times pointless lives speculating- "Do I really love her?", "I think there is something wrong with my metabolism.", "Why would he say that?". They unfortunately die before they have answers to most of these pointless and overrated questions.

AF471657

Uncertainty seems to be as certain as birth and death in most human lives. James is one of these people. Naturally, he does not have answers to most of the questions he asks himself. Which person his age does? He is, however, entirely and unequivocally certain of one thing: there is something severely wrong with him. This virus that eats away at his soul is getting stronger. This sickness, this malignancy, it tears away at his thirst to live and his passions. It grows with every waking minute. Thoughts are its air, solitude: its food. It starts off rather small: a single word that you hear and nobody else does. It grows inside of you uncontrollably, an impure baby that sucks on your thoughts, ingests your hopes and dreams until you merely become a vessel for it. This virus, this beautiful sickness silently destroys so many souls. There is no more slow and cruel fate on this planet than the onset of insanity.

The high-pitched, incessant voices of Michael and Veronica downstairs begin to arouse irritation in James. He hates his father's voice. He hates his fake smiles, he hates the scent of his cheap cologne that causes James so many headaches, he hates the clueless and naive look his father always has on his unkempt face. He hates everything about him. "Jamie! Veronica made you waffles," yells his father from downstairs. James dislikes it when his father is kind to him. "I'll be right down, Michael!" Ever since the night it happened, James always calls his father by his first name in a sort of objection to being this cowardly man's son. He stumbles to his bathroom, his bare feet dragging along the varnished wood that is his floor. The reflection of his face bothers him- he looks very much like her. The thought of living through another day makes him cringe as he brushes his teeth. "Fuck Johannesburg."

Downstairs on the sofa, his father and stepmother are perched in front of the flat-screen television. James thinks to himself how people are actually no different than the animals they cage: the only thing that really separates them from the savages they look down on is the ability to shamelessly judge each other. "Good morning Veronica. Good morning Michael." His tone is almost rehearsed. "Your breakfast is on the kitchen counter, darling," his stepmother says to him in her shrill voice.

James wonders what she sees in his father, "Maybe she's a gold-digger," he thinks and immediately shrugs off the notion remembering what a miser his father is. She is wearing denim shorts and the revealing pink tank-top that James attempted to hide once, as he believes it in not age appropriate for her nor flattering to her full form. If the circumstances had been different, he might have actually liked this feisty woman. Reluctant to do so, he begins to eat his breakfast. Veronica's cooking has always been sub-standard: if her meal is not under-cooked, it resembles charcoal. This morning, she drowned his waffles in maple syrup in an attempt to veil the putrid taste of her effortless cuisine. "Do you like it, honey?" she asks her stepson. Her words of endearment seem condescending to the arrogant, and motherly to the insecure. "Thank you, Veronica." James, regardless of his contemptible opinions of most people in his life and his increasing mental instability, has always had a polite nature. "Are you ready for that Othello test today, son?" his father asks him, as he places his long arm over his bride's shoulder and pulls her towards him, kissing her forehead. This was, essentially, what breakfast comprised of in the Stevens' household: exchanging pleasantries between gulping down unpleasant food, awkward silences that rear their heads ever so frequently and the unspoken words that make the air ever so dense with frustration. "I think I'll do fine." He knows he didn't bother to prepare for it, instead, he spent the night fantasizing about death. He desperately hopes his instability is a phase and ignores his better judgment. "I'm worried about you, son. Mr. Matthews called and told me you're not showing any interest in your school work." Calmly standing up, James walks towards the wooden front door of their upper middle-class estate. "I'll be in the car." He exits the suburban house, imagining how his life might have turned out if his father was more of a man, or if his mother had not died of her illness.

James feels an immense amount of guilt for what he has just done as he slowly paces towards his father's beat down 1984 Ford. "You act like this because it is the only way to prevent yourself from going postal" he re-affirms himself. It is not very convincing. The drizzling rain is soothing. Mr. Clarke is mowing his lawn with gusto. At the sight of this colossal man, James wishes he had a father like Mr. Clarke: an authority figure he could feel respect for instead of pity. "Good morning, young man," yells this robust gentleman from across the road and waves with the chauvinistic pride that most alpha males possess. Two beads of sweat make their way down his bushy blonde eyebrows to his long inwardly caved nose. "He looks like a wife-beater," James thinks to himself with a smirk before waving back at him, feigning nonchalance. Seconds later, he notices his father opening the driver's door of the blue-gray car. "What a meek man my father is," thinks James to himself, simultaneously admiring the bold masculinity that was Mr. Clarke. He tears his eyes away from his neighbour's front lawn and enters the barely road-worthy vehicle he is resting his weight on. Danielle nicknamed this car 'The Abomination' the previous week when James's father had picked them up from afternoon detention. Michael pulls cautiously out of the driveway, as if it were a process so delicate that if it were to be done slightly incorrectly, it would result in the destruction of all mankind.

The Ford pulls up in front of the automated black gates of Breakwater High. "Do you need any money?"; "A twenty will be fine, thanks." The image of James fleeing the car reminds his father of a man he once saw being released from prison. The awkward feeling that filled the car seconds ago dissipates as Michael watches his son walk away from him. Michael hopes that just this once, his son will look back at him and wave like he used to when he was younger. No luck. James walks with immense presence, almost arrogance. Michael remembers the kind-natured, shy boy who just a few years back (or it seems so to him?) was starting his first day of elementary school, waving furiously with joy emanating from his face as he walked into the rainbow-painted door of his kindergarten classroom. Instead of nostalgia filling Michael, he is overcome by a strong sense of mourning for the death of the boy his son once was, the boy that once was his son, before he became this semi-mute basket case. James's mother always knew what to say and do to keep her son in line. Her son smiled when she was alive, the fire had not left his eyes when she was there. After she had departed, James slipped into a frenzy of self-destruction. Michael feels responsible for not providing enough help to his ex-wife while he still could, before her sickness took her away from them. He also regrets not being there for their son after she died. Michael loves Veronica, he truly does. Her kindness and non-confrontational nature has been the best thing that could have happened to their family after such a dramatic death. However, the fact still remains: every woman, no matter how amazing she may be, comes second to the awesomeness that was Kate Rodger-Stevens. "James is so much like her," Michael thinks to himself. He has her light blue eyes and her demeanor of unparalleled superiority. All Michael got from his father is his gender. The stoic presence that Kate possessed has recently become apparent in her son. Michael starts the vehicle and drives off, half hoping a drunken driver will prevent him from reaching his place of work.

CHAPTER II (SYLVIA)

Martin casually jogs down Main Road as he does every day when the sun is about to set. He thinks of how his vacation is coming to an end and how this inevitably means his return to teaching at Breakwater High. He loathes every brick of that building and every 'bastard child' (which he is convinced is as a result of incest) that he has to teach again soon. He has taught there for eight years already, and he believes he is yet to teach a delinquent that has potential to become something exceptional. "I guess we're all out of Einsteins and Shakespeares," he thinks to himself with his panting separating the fluency of his bitter thoughts. He regrets his choice of career deeply. He always wanted to be a teacher: he believed he could do his part in the world by helping to shape the leaders of tomorrow. This dream came to an abrupt halt when he began to realise that these leaders were nowhere to be seen. As he jogs, he avoids tiny cracks in the ground, sub-consciously counting the number of steps he takes. 754, 755, 756... The beauty of London amazes him. The regal buildings and the atmosphere of chilled industrial production entices a deeper part of his being. He considers moving here for a few moments, and then decides against it. "I hate the fucking rain," he thinks to himself. Exhausted, he staggers to the nearest bench. "What a beautiful view," he thinks to himself. His seat on the mahogany-painted cement bench overlooks a most magnificent lake. It is moments like this that re-affirms Nicholas's belief in a God. "Such beauty can only be designed by the Almighty," he thinks while looking through his canary-yellow backpack beside him for his pack of cigarettes. His search is interrupted by a horrifying sight. On this most majestic lake, about 120 metres away from him, floats a large object: Lifeless. It is a woman. Alarmed by this, Martin rushes toward her, hoping she is still alive. He knows it is absurd to believe this lady, wearing only a loose fitting T-shirt and silk shorts, could survive the arctic waters of wintery London for longer than a few minutes. As he runs as fast as he can in this fatigued state, his mind softly curses her for interrupting his rest. He feels guilty immediately thereafter. Every muscle of his athletic body flexes until he runs beyond his optimum speed. He dives into the icy pool and spends a matter of seconds hauling her out. He cannot feel how heavy she is, or how cold the water is: all he can feel is the unfiltered adrenalin coursing through his veins- it allows him to accomplish this Herculean task. He places her on the mahogany bench, and calls the ambulance immediately. To the untrained eye, she is a corpse.

*　　*　　*

"Jesus, lady! Don't scare us like that ever again," voices Jack, with a sigh of relief and a kind smile on his face. He looks at the woman whose life he had just saved. Her half open eyes pierce through the wet, black-velvet that is her hair and as she looks directly at Jack's teary ones. Today is his sixth day as an intern at Mercy Hospital. "You nearly drowned, miss. If a young man jogging by didn't find you, you'd be dead." Jack's unhealthy emotional attachment to people, especially his patients, is as a result of his many experiences with loss and pain. He went straight from high school to medical school, and he did not allow himself to date after the death of his high school sweetheart in their junior year. His thoughts are interrupted by this middle aged woman's outburst. "Ted must be worried sick about me! Please, can I go?" Jack asks for her name to which she replies: "My name is Sylvia. Sylvia Plath". The year is 2005.

CHAPTER III (SYLVIA)

Weeks have passed since this wrinkled, slender framed woman had been admitted into Mercy Hospital's psychiatric ward. In this time, Dr. Jack Smith visited her daily. She stares blankly at the sour faced nurse as she, the nurse, tries to remember what medication had been assigned to Sylvia for the day. "What an ugly hippo," Sylvia thinks to herself and begins to laugh uncontrollably. The nurse, though frustrated, takes this opportunity to force the multi-coloured capsules down her patient's wide throat. Sylvia gags slightly, and then swallows. She gulps down large quantities of water to get the synthetic taste of plastic out of her mouth. "Nurse, I know you all think I'm unstable, but I really don't belong here. I'm fine! Ted must be so worried about me." Her tone is so convincing, it is as if she is merely stating a fact. "I know honey," says the nurse patronisingly, "Now let's get you to bed." Sylvia hates being mothered. She wants to leave, but she is afraid of what might happen if she gets caught. The medication begins to take its effect on her. She has become fond of its calming effect. She calls it her 'release from reality'. In this state of mind, merely existing is pleasurable. Nothing matters to her, not love, not pain, nothing. In this state, she knows she is not Sylvia Plath, and that Sylvia Plath was just her favourite poet before she somehow decided to become her. She will forget this truth when she is lucid again. The medication will not help her remember who she is either. This does not bother her though, because in this state, this state of sheer ecstasy, absolutely nothing matters.

The stout nurse curses in her Russian tongue as she helps this patient place herself on the linen sheets of the single bed. The bed is hard, but Sylvia cannot feel it. A silhouette in a white coat appears beside her bed, blocking some of the light from entering through the glass window beside which she rests. Sylvia, even in her half-conscious state knows who this saintly looking gentleman is. The smell of his cologne is the only pleasant smell she has known in the past few weeks. "How is she today, Agatha?" asks Dr. Smith. His register is soothing and his tone almost shy. His reserved, and almost clingy nature is what makes

Sylvia so comfortable around this insecure man. "No improvement Jack. She still can't remember her name, her age. Completely nothing." The intoxicated woman can detect the frustration in her care-taker's voice. "What a bitch," Sylvia thinks to herself, attempting without success to form a more vulgar word aloud. Jack strokes her arm after hearing her mumble. These moments of cruel rage Sylvia has, drugged or not, is a true reflection of what Sylvia was like the weeks before she was plunged into the dark sea of uncertainty.

* * *

Agatha's departure is a relief to the now conscious Sylvia. For some odd reason, her lunacy is at its peak during the hours after the medication wears off. She sits up and stares out the window, looks 12 floors down into the moonlit gardens of this London hospital. This patient's first suicide attempt, like her idol's, was unsuccessful. In her mind, this weathered woman is now reliving the days of Sylvia Plath before her second suicide attempt, the successful one.

This moment is her insanity. This moment of idle thought,

believing she is another woman, *that* is her insanity. What this woman does not know is that she is days away from becoming insane again, this time mimicking the downfall of the dead woman she believes she is, the poetic mastermind she has now, in her mind, become. This is essentially what madness is- it is a cure to unbearable pain, a cure to unsurpassable misery. The human mind becomes so unhappy with its sad reality, that it breaks itself to form a new impersonal one.

It feels like days before the sun sets before her hazel eyes. The elegance of the sky changing completely in a matter of moments amazes her. She feels inspired. She frantically searches underneath her bed for the empty book and the black fountain-pen Jack had sneaked into her room and she begins to write in it:

"The Arrival of the Bee Box, by Sylvia Plath..."

CHAPTER IV (JAMES)

"The Arrival of the Bee Box," Mr. Matthews begins reading to his tenth grade English class, "By Sylvia Plath."

"I ordered this, clean wood box

Square as a chair and almost too heavy to lift.

I would say it was the coffin of a midget

Or a square baby

Were there not such a din in it."

James smiles to himself. This has become his favourite poem as of recent. He recites it to himself every night before he falls asleep (or in most cases, tries to fall asleep). He begins to mouth the words as his teacher continues to passionately recite it.

"The box is locked, it is dangerous.

I had to live with it overnight

And I can't keep away from it.

There are no windows, so I can't see what is in there.

There is only a little grid, no exit.

I put my eye to the grid.

It is dark, dark,

With the swarmy feeling of African hands

Minute and shrunk for export,

Black on black, angrily clambering."

The class clown points at the only black learner in that classrrom, and five of the inhabitants of the room begin to giggle. Nicholas Matthews gives them a stern look that silences them. He looks back at the book in his pale, aged hands and continues to read.

"How can I let them out?

It is the noise that appalls me most of all,

The unintelligible syllables.

It is like a Roman mob,

Small, taken one by one, but my god, together!

I lay my ear to furious Latin.

I am not a Caesar.

I have simply ordered a box of maniacs.

They can be sent back.

They can die, I need feed them nothing, I am the owner."

"It, insanity, is the owner," James casually thinks to himself, "And there is no way of sending it back."

"I wonder how hungry they are.

I wonder if they would forget me

If I just undid the locks and stood back and turned into a tree.

There is the laburnum, its blond colonnades,

And the petticoats of cherry.

They might ignore me immediately

In my moon and suit funeral veil.

I am no source of honey

So why would they turn on me?

Tomorrow I will be sweet God, I will set the free.

The box is only temporary."

Nicholas looks up and notices three amazed or impressed faces from the 22 that stare back at him. He sighs to himself and mentally asks himself how somebody who can hear and understand English cannot be moved by such intense writing. "Or they are just too dense to understand any of it," he thinks. He looks around his classroom again, optimistic to find an overt reaction (he did give them a minute to think about what they had just heard), knowing he is unlikely to find one. Sarah Alexander is brushing her auburn hair and tying it up in a single platted ponytail that rests on her right shoulder. She thinks of her college boyfriend who she will be seeing after this. Bradley Denham slyly adjusts his shoulder-length hair to shadow the earphones in his abnormally large ears. Vulgar rap vibrates his eardrums. Alfred Jude is fingering his ears and tasting what he finds. Six years from now he will die of stomach cancer (completely unrelated). "Christ," the English teacher thinks in frustration, his eyes making their way to the clock that hangs on the white wall at the back of the room. "The period will end in a moment. Danielle and James, come speak to me at the end of the lesson." The bell rings.

James shoves his weighty textbooks in bag and flings it over him to lazily rest on his left shoulder-blade. He assumes he knows why he is being summoned by this ancient man. He pushes his chair into the desk and begins to make his way to the table at the front of the classroom where his superior is seated aristocratically. "It's last week's test," James thinks to himself, knowing he failed it. He notices Danielle attempting to make a dash for it. "Danielle Augustus!" Mr. Matthews shouts, bringing this unusually dressed girl's escape to a halt. Danielle, feeling humiliated, scratches the scalp her blue hair is rooted to. The two young adults position themselves in front of their summoner, looking him dead in the eye. "I assume you both know why you're here," begins Nicholas, in his deep tone of voice. "So you can pretend to be a real teacher and lecture us?" asks the blue-haired girl sarcastically. Danielle, in summary, is every right-wing, conservative parent's worst nightmare. She recently moved down from London with more tattoos scattered across her pale body than there are people who in some of her classes. This, in conjunction with her tendency to wear only black clothing with skulls or weaponry printed on it, would render most parents speechless. "You both failed your Othello exam last week," the stoic educator continues, ignoring Danielle's jibe, "If you have any desire not to fail my course this semester, you will write an essay on the poem we discussed in class today and you will slip it under my door first thing tomorrow morning. I have already phoned your parents." Danielle rolls her eyes (she has red contact lenses on) and storms out whispering "Fuck you," slamming the wooden door behind her. Mr. Matthews pretends that he did not hear it. He has spent 28 years teaching, and in this time he has had to deal with many youngsters like Danielle. He forgives most of their follies because he pities the 95% of them who make nothing of themselves and he admires the 5% with the strength to. "You're dismissed."

Outside, James spots his friend leaning with her back against the wall and her feet about 1.5 feet in front of her, in a typical Bowie pose, puffing away at her joint. "How do you sneak that shit in here?" comments James, seating himself on the floor beside Danielle. They spend the next three minutes passing the cannabis to and fro, each inhaling its smoke deeply. "You should just do the stupid essay," starts James, "Your family have enough to worry about." Six weeks ago, Danielle's brother had been diagnosed with skin cancer. Ever since, he has been in hospital getting treatment. His flowing blonde hair has begun to fall out, the unblemished porcelain that was once his skin is now dented with disease. Danielle slowly nods at the suggestion, exhales a cloud of smoke and turns her face away. James can almost smell the teardrops meeting with Danielle's prominent eyeliner. Sobbing sounds become apparent to him. "Danielle, look at me." James hates to see her like this. He misses the shameless rebellion that he was so attracted to. He wipes the tears away from her and offers her a smile (James seldom smiles). "It will be okay. You need to be strong for your mom and brother." James begins to weep remembering how depression eventually took his mother away from him. They kiss passionately for a moment. "I love you". Danielle stands up to leave. "I love you too."

CHAPTER V (JAMES)

He gazes at the time. "Almost midnight," James lazily announces to himself, tearing himself away from his comfortable bed, placing himself on the uncomfortable wooden chair in front of his working desk. He is at his worst when it is late at night. The darkness of the midnight air contributes to the madness he is gradually and inevitably slipping into. In his mind, he begins to weigh up whether or not he should in fact write the essay he was requested to. "So what if I repeat a year?" he asks himself, hoping it did not sound as depressing as it did. He had no choice. He lifts the black fountain-pen on his desk, remembering the day his mother had given it to him: four days before she had died in the bathtub of their old home. He was certain that what would eventually take his mother away from him was the chain-smoking habit she picked up in high school. He prepared himself for years to accept her death after the doctor spotted the first signs of lung cancer. The third doctor who treated her finally 'cured' her of it, only for another sickness to take her weeks thereafter, just after her son began to believe he might actually have his mother at his graduation. A single teardrop rolls down from his bloodshot eyes. He begins to write.

An hour passes and all he has before him is half a page of drivel. He does not have the strength to write anymore, so he makes his way downstairs for a glass of water. He opens the shoulder-tall green fridge. Nothing he wants is in there. He can hear his father and stepmother down the hall whispering dirty things to each other. He feels repulsed from the pit of his stomach. Every moment to this young man feels like he is not really himself. Like he is an actor in a television show he has no interest in being a part of. He decides to use this feeling, this feeling of utter hopelessness as a fuel for the essay he is now going to finally write.

*　　*　　*

Mr. Matthews enters his classroom to find two pieces of paper on his floor. Looking at his watch, he decides he has time to grade one of them before the staff meeting.

James Stevens - The

Arrival of the Bee Box

In this poem, Plath talks about the mental illness she had that eventually drove her to taking her own life. The 'bee box' symbolises this illness: her insanity. In this essay I will focus on attempting to describe what insanity feels like through the eyes of Sylvia.

Insanity gives no warning before it arrives. It's a new feeling, you're not sure what it is, but you're fascinated by it. The fascination soon begins to disappear, you begin to realize what this new parcel, this 'bee box' in your mind is. At first, you refuse to accept that it is what it is: you try to make excuses and give different names to it. It buzzes like a swarm of bees, like a drone that won't shut up! You can't silence it, you can't even understand it. It is a disease; no medicine can detect it, no sure way of treating it. Even if you do manage to fix it, you will probably die of one of its ripple effects.

You want to set this sickness free, out of your body. It grows and grows until you see it in every facet of your life. The father who could once do no wrong makes you want to club in his head.

School, friends, everything just stops having meaning. The mundane nature of your entire life becomes apparent; reality is just not enough anymore. You think you can fix it, you believe you are 'the owner'; you even believe that you are 'sweet God' and you can set these noisy bees in your mind free. You soon realise how powerless you are. Your actions aren't yours anymore. The bees swarm around your every thought, pollinating it with ideas of hurting yourself, of hurting others.

The arrival of the bee box is not only the arrival of her madness, but also the arrival of her death. It is a scarlet letter from God: you are unsure of the nature of your crime, but you know you will be stoned to death for it- by yourself.

The bee box is her green light to suicide.

Sickness can sometimes be a gift. Asperger's syndrome allows those who have it to be extremely logical at the cost of their social competence. In the same way, depression and insanity (which can often be two different stages of the same thing) grants her victim supreme artistic abilities in exchange for longevity. She is a merciless seductress that steals souls, shatters families and leaves behind her a trail of artworks that will be admired for centuries by those that were too commonplace to be touched by her.

A single droplet of water forms on the inner edge of Nicholas's right eye. This is the best piece of work he was handed all year. The words he had just read continue to swirl around his head. They were beautiful. It was raw emotion: unfiltered art. He grades it and heads to his imminent meeting, wiping his cheeks. Nicholas did not know that every word he had just read was how the young man in question actually felt. His confusion, his helplessness so poignantly conveyed in a page and a half of prose. Nicholas had not known that he had just peeked into James Stevens' beebox.

*   *   *

A week has passed and James's condition increases in severity as the seconds fade away. Everything begins to look unfamiliar. The bed he lies on feels different. Every word he speaks, every action done by this foreign body he is trapped in seems meaningless. The fracture in his mind is gradually and inevitably becoming the puppet master, the ring leader in this circus that is his life. The feeling of dull shock follows him everywhere, accompanied by a caged rage that fights relentlessly to break the titanium chains that are James's heartstrings. His body is in combat with his mind. 04h23 and he cannot sleep. It is the voices that keep him up. "The devil's henchmen," James calls them, “It is like they don't want me to sleep so my suffering is continuous."

He surrenders to his sleepless fate, moving to his desk to record his feelings in his journal.

CHAPTER VI (SYLVIA)

Time is the biggest torture for Sylvia. Her condition might have been slightly less unbearable if she were not cooped up in this hospital to inertly drink in every second. Agatha helps her get dressed for breakfast. This job is not suited for this perpetually bitter woman. She wanted to be a supermodel when she was a beautiful four year old, posing for hours in front of the mirror, pretending to take pictures of herself on her Barbie pink plastic camera. The beauty of food was learnt by her not too long after this, shattering any dreams she had of being on the cover of Russian Vogue. Agatha looks at this fast aging woman. "She must have been beautiful," the plump woman thinks to herself, almost pitiful of her patient's fast fading youth. "Agatha, when do they plan on letting me go? I'm quite sick of this place," says Sylvia, pushing one lock of hair behind her ear.

Dr. Smith takes his seat on Sylvia's bed, beside her. "Jack, how much longer before you all let me leave?" she asks him. His eyebrows frown; he thinks desperately to himself how he should approach this most delicate topic. Agatha, certain of what is about to happen, evades. "You are not well, Sylvia." "Of course I'm well, look at me! Do I look sick or crazy to you?" She is angered by his statement. In her mind, she is certain of her mental and physical health. "Why do all of you think I'm crazy?" Sylvia asks him, grabbing his right arm, her eyes desperate for some answers, answers that the man before her has been avoiding to give her for weeks. He now knows he has to give her truth. "You're not Sylvia Plath," he finally says, half afraid of what her response may be. "What? I don't understand." She is baffled. "You are not Sylvia Plath," he continues, "You are very sick and we need to treat you." "Are you listening to yourself, doctor? I'm not sick! Look at me, Jack!" The doctor pauses for a moment, searching his thoughts furiously for something to say before realising that there is no right thing to say in this most unfortunate moment. “I’m sorry, Elizabeth,” he says to her before walking away reluctantly. It is in this instant that Sylvia sees the truth that was in front of her the entire time: this institution is not her prison, her mind is.

CHAPTER VII (JAMES)

It is 06h00. James springs purposefully out of his bed as the alarm clock serenades his auditory sense. He trips momentarily as he leaps to open his curtains to let the sunlight in, chuckling at his clumsy nature in the mornings. Today, for the first time in a very long time, he had a reason to wake up. He continues to go about preparing for his day with a sincere smile on his face the entire time. Today, he knew for an absolute fact that it would end better than yesterday did. He knew that today will be the first day in a long time that he will not feel constantly miserable because one thing separates this specific day from the countless before it. Today, he had something that he actually wanted to do.

As James walks downstairs, the voices of his guardians grow louder and louder. He can tell that they are watching early morning sitcoms again. “Good morning Veronica, Good morning Michael.” They respond warmly. “What’s for breakfast today? I’m starved.” James continues. Veronica points to the coffee table where there lay her attempt at making muffins- it appears severely under-baked. James reluctantly takes one and washes each bite down with a sip of coffee. “Mr. Matthews called to tell me how impressed he was with your essay.” Michael says before taking another bite of his bride’s handiwork. “I’m glad,” James says with an ever-so-subtle smile. His father had not seen that in years. It was a pleasant surprise.

On the way to school, Michael and his son spoke a bit more than they usually do. He even managed to get a chuckle or two out of the handsome young man that he was chauffeuring. The atmosphere in the car was almost pleasant. After another fifteen minutes of travel, they finally reach James’ place of study. Michael, happy to have bonded with his son a bit today, gave him double the pocket money he usually does. “Thanks Dad,” James says before swiftly leaving the car on hearing the school bell. Those two words stirred such emotion in this mild-natured, mildly wrinkled man. Like he does every morning, Michael watches his son as he makes his way to the large gates of Breakwater High School. He notices, for the first time in over a decade, a bit of himself in his son. Somewhere amidst that Kate aura that swirls fiercely around him is a touch of Michael- a subtle submissive kind of glow. As Michael pulls out of the parking lot, he notices his son turn around and wave at him. He waves back at him before wiping a teardrop off of his quivering cheek.

*   *   *

Michael and Veronica make a speedy entry into the driveway of their cosy, double-story home. The winter air is especially cold this dusk. They rush into the house, Michael trying his best not to drop the groceries. Today has been a good day for them both, especially him. As he places the parcels on the kitchen counter, Michael notices a note with his son's handwriting on it reading:

"I tried. Choosing life is too hard after all that I have been through, dad. I chose peace."

www.ingramcontent.com/pod-product-compliance
Ingram Content Group UK Ltd.
Pitfield, Milton Keynes, MK11 3LW, UK
UKHW041901190726
13854UKWH00003B/1026

9 781105 829161